the outside looking in. I don't hold you responsible in any way."

Pygge sighed.

"Sir, Tostig has told me who you think is the culprit and I have to say I was shocked. I've known the man a long time."

"Aye ... he's very... plausible."

"Just to let you know, sir. He comes from Cadley. He's a freeman of the town, son of a freeman: not one of your folk but he was born and bred there. He'll know every inch of the place."

"That accounts for his knowledge of the underground passage."

"And of course he's related...."

"Yes. I know. That fact threw me for a while. But now I see clearly what happened."

I moved to the door. "I'm off for some pie. No doubt some will find its way to you both soon. Tonight we set a trap. Enjoy your pie and I hope that later tomorrow I can come and tell you, Henry, we've caught our killer. If you're at home Tostig, I'll see you there."

"Take care sir," said Tostig, concern written on his face once more.

"I shall Tostig. Good afternoon gentlemen."

*****

I ate a healthy slice of Agnes' pie at dinner and chatted to Johannes who came back in shortly after I left Tostig and Pygge.

I asked after Pygge's injury.

"I can't tell you yet if the leg will mend. There's fearful burning and so much skin and flesh is missing. I've seen infection and gangrene set in quickly to such wounds. Keeping it clean and relatively dry but cool is of the essence. A poultice of diluted vinegar, honey and lavender is the best thing, I find."

"He's very stoic."

"Aye, the pain is formidable but I have managed to mix some numbing potion with the poultice. I hope that goes some way to helping. He's taken a pain killing remedy too. He sleeps much of the time which is just as well. Tostig will go home today with Hal, I think. Best Alysoun looks after him. I can then concentrate on Henry."

"Tostig has told me how the place managed to be set on fire. He blames himself."

"I know. Last night he was raving about it. I had a devil of a job to calm him."

"The church is gone but the stone crypt, or whatever it is, is still there."

"He tried to describe what he saw in the dark and by the light of a stub of a candle. It sounded like nothing I have ever seen."

"When we go back to look, come with us. It will be interesting, I think."

"Aye, I will," said Johannes.

The doctor stretched. "You'll rebuild the church I suppose? In stone?"

"What else can I do? The folk around have nowhere to worship now. Durley is too far. Marlborough is too far. Especially for the aged and infirm. Let's call it my penance. My good works. My grandfather and great grandfather built the churches at Durley and Bedwyn. I've built nothing yet. Perhaps Cadley will be my monument."

Johannes laughed. "But it will not house your bones. You are too rooted in Durley."

"Who knows where my bones will lie, Johannes?"

"Aye, none of us can really know that."

"The King may call us up for duty. I might die on a sodden French field with an arrow in my back"

Johannes guffawed. "Never! All your wounds will be in the front. I know you!"

"Let's hope you'll be there to minister to me then."

No, Paul. You are quite right. I didn't die. I'm still here, praise be to God, and telling you my tales.

*****

Hal came in just after dinner and mounted Tostig on plodding old Coro. I told him who I thought our murderer was and what we were about to do to catch him.

"You be careful, lad," he said. "You might think him a soft man but we know he's handy with knife and bow and he's wily and resourceful."

"I'll have help, Hal."

My man at arms nodded and started off for home. A couple of the other grooms had come with him as an escort. They would make sure that there was no further attempt on anyone's life.

Surely now, our culprit knew what Tostig had imparted to me? Perhaps he was counting on me not understanding.

The afternoon passed slowly. I sent Stephen and Peter into the town to the house of our felon to search. They came back with plenty of evidence, and some forged coin. We also found the trussel of the forged die. I gave them to Gayle and he locked them in his office.

Gradually the work in the castle ceased. The masons came down from their walls; the to-ing and fro-ing of the couriers and messengers slowed; the supplies coming in dried to a trickle. Those who didn't belong in the castle overnight went home. Andrew Merriman took over from FitzAlan and prepared to take the night guard.

I scratched once more on Gayle's office door and poked my head around it.

"Pete, shall we meet quietly at the south west tower, by the moat just around dark? Best we all go in ones and twos I think. I don't want the killer to know we are massing there."

"Who have we got?"

"Andrew, me, you and my two men at arms."

Gayle nodded.

"I'll go first," I said.

I wandered out of the castle gate and said goodnight to the gate guard.

Andrew had briefed him that we would be back in later.

Once again, I jumped down onto the boggy ground by the drawbridge and scurried around the wall. This time I rounded the furthest tower and waited.

My nose picked up the terrible scent of human waste and I looked up in the gloom. There a few feet above me was the chute of the garderobe of the end of the guard room.

I moved a little way forward of it.

Andrew came next and was followed shortly by my two men at arms, Stephen and Peter. The last to arrive was Gayle.

We whispered amongst ourselves.

"Maybe you two," I pointed to my men, "should wait by the bridge and when you detect our man coming, let him get in front of you, then come up behind him. He'll not be able to run back and evade us."

Stephen and Peter nodded and dashed back the way they had come.

After a short while of quiet, "Can we all swim?" I asked. I knew Andrew could swim though not quite as well as I could.

"Aye, I can swim," said Gayle. "I grew up in London by the Thames. You had to be able to swim."

I was scanning the end of the wall, peering into the gloom for any sign of our man.

"Good. One of us might end up in the moat," I chuckled quietly.

I turned back to Peterkin. "I didn't know you grew up by the Thames."

"Aye, My father was a Thames waterman."

"Well, well," I said. "Then a moat should prove no problem for you."

Gayle stifled a laugh. "Nevertheless, I don't want to be the one to fall in the drink."

"Shh… Here comes our man, as I thought."

I heard a scuffling as the man descended the now dark drawbridge. It had not been drawn up for many years now but was left down day and night. In times of war or threat it would be drawn up at night. It was however checked regularly.

The flares held by the soldiers on the upper walls flickered. I could just make out a man, bent double, tripping lightly along the boggy ground. He struck a light and lit the stub of a candle. The flame's light caught his face and sent the pattern of it into sharp angles.

There was no sign of Peter or Stephen.

I waited for the man to bend to his work of finding the metal which had been thrown from the window. He searched. He swore. He stood and stared out over the dark moat. Then he took a few steps further on and began again, once more bent double.

I stepped out from the corner of the tower base.

"So Luke, good evening, it's nice to meet you at last. You won't find what you've come to look for, by the way."

The man dropped his candle stub.

Gayle pushed close to me at the tower side, Andrew stood a little way behind me. I could see, by the light of the castle flares, Stephen and Peter stealthily creeping up the path behind our felon.

"Oh Sir Aumary, you gave me a turn. Yes, I lost a cloak brooch a little while ago and I thought to come and see if it was here. I wondered if I'd lost it when I was here fishing. What are you doing here?"

"Nice try, but you know full well I was waiting, we are waiting for you."

"Why ever would you do that?"

I fished in my scrip. "This the brooch you lost, Luke?"

I saw the man's eyes take in the small metal bar reflected in the light of our lantern. There was no hesitation. "What's that, sir?"

"The last piece of metal which Beecroft stole for you from the forge in the castle, and which he left here for you to recover. Elswith saw you both that day when she came to town to bring her spinning to the weavers."

"Oh no sir, not me."

The man known as Luke looked back and saw my two men at arms.

"What's this all about, sir?"

"Perhaps we should go up to the Lord Neville's office and I can tell you what I think this is all about," I said.

"If that is what you want, m'lord," said our felon, unperturbed.

I nodded to Stephen who took hold of the man and checked him for weapons. I saw a knife flash in the light of the flare as Stephen took it from him and stuffed it into his belt.

Flanked by Peter and Stephen we marched our man back into the castle and up to de Neville's office. Gayle went before us and opened the door. Only once did the man look back at those following him, and finally we collected in the middle of the room.

Gayle moved the few lamps placed around the room and one or two lanterns which were left here and there. These would be lit in bad weather when the light became too poor for any clerk working there.

Gayle stood by the door with my two men at arms. Andrew worked his way to the furthest table and sat on the edge. I stood and folded my arms over my chest. The man known as Luke stood in the centre of the room and the guards vacated and stood outside. Then we locked the door.

"So tell me - Beecroft? He was the man who stole the metal for the dies for you?"

"I'm sorry, sir. I knew the man but I knew nothing about him stealing any metal. He was a farrier and I don't know too many people from the stable."

"He sat beneath a window and fished." I gestured to the outer window.

"I joined him now and again on a good day. It's very pleasant sitting out there in the sunshine."

"He didn't fish. You collected what he threw out or maybe he passed to it you."

"No sir." He shook his head.

"You told me that you weighed all the silver. It wasn't possible, you said, to lose any. All the tiny pieces were collected together and reused. Yes. By you. And because the silver is yours it didn't matter a jot. You adulterated that silver with copper and made coins with a forged die, one which did not come from London."

"You had us all," said Gayle. "We believed everything you said."

"Why should we not, Pete?" I said. "He was in a position of trust for many years. He bribed and threatened others into helping him and then when they became too unreliable, he killed them. Others knew he was a murderer and became afraid."

"I have killed no one."

"Elswith Larkworthy, Beecroft, Carrier; you attempted to kill me and my man Tostig and you did kill my worker Kineman."

"No sir. You are mistaken." He flashed his perfect white teeth at us, made for a bench and sat down.

"My only crime, if crime it is, was to fail to know of the stealing of the iron from the blacksmith's forge to make a die. How would I know? But someone, as you say, has been cleverly stealing it and taking it from the castle. I see that now. There are many men working here. Any one of them could have stolen it. How was I to know someone had the skill to forge a die?"

"But only you could have used it. You needed that metal. No one else had the skills to engrave the die. I beg to argue with you, Luke; your only mistake was to make it in reverse. Not being used to making such things and being used to seeing the fruits of your labours with the sceptre on the right side, you copied what you saw. How long did it take for someone to work out that the coins you issued were wrong?"

I saw Peterkin shaking his head.

I smiled at Crosscastle, for the moneyer was indeed our felon. "Luke. Oh you thought yourself so clever, didn't you?"

"I wonder why you keep calling me that, sir. You know my name is Edwig."

"Luke? Several people have heard you called Luke. It's a sort of nickname about the castle isn't it? Luke. But what people really heard was 'lucrum' wasn't it. Money. Latin for money, profit. They wouldn't know that word. They'd make it into Luke for that was a word they'd understand."

Crosscastle scowled. "If you say so, sir."

"It all began with Beecroft, smuggling metal from the castle forge at the stables through the window. He procured the metal for you so that you could engrave the dies. No one would find anything on his person. You would go out to the moat and sit, idly feeding the fish, or was it ducks?"

"Ducks, sir? Yes." Again the white smile lit up his face. "I like to feed them. They are very interesting creatures."

"You fed Beecroft with silver ingots. He took them home, flattened them out and with a punch which you had made, fabricated some forged coins. Together you made them. Beecroft only had the bottom of the die. You, Crosscastle, had the top. Both of you were needed to make them. A lack of trust I'd say. You didn't trust Beecroft with both parts, did you?"

Crosscastle was silent.

"We found those coins. Not good ones, but they might be mistaken for old degraded ones of King Henry's reign as long as they were not scrutinised too closely. They would do to pass about the town for this and that. Beecroft couldn't resist spending a couple in the town, could he? You, however, were saving yours. Too risky in the town. You'd amass a good few and then you'd go elsewhere to spend them, or perhaps you'd be off, never to be seen again. Never quite had enough though, did you? Always wanted more." We found them by the way... the coins and the die."

Crosscastle jumped up. "You've been to my house... my wife..."

"Steady, man," said Stephen, tensing. "I don't like sudden movements. I'm rather like Bunce in that way... I get a bit nervy with me knife."

"You should have thought of that, Crosscastle," I said.

He stared around at us all. Suddenly the white smile was gone. He sat down again.

"So there you are taking out your silver and collecting the iron when who should come tripping along the path but your cousin Elswith on her way into town. I'm not sure how she realised what you were doing but she probably saw you and Beecroft by the moat. Maybe more than once. Maybe she overheard you? Did she see you give Beecroft a die? Did she realise that the die should not leave your person? Had you told her that at some point in the past?

"Maybe she tackled you about it. You denied it. She was certain. She was going to report you. And on that day when she was about to go into town again, before you were to go to your job at the castle, you took a rouncey from the stable and went up to the downs to reason with her." I paced about a little and peeked into the small space which housed the garderobe.

"Did you offer her money?"

"Stupid bitch," said Crosscastle at a whisper.

"I suppose she said she wouldn't take any."

The man clamped his lips together again.

"And so you strangled her. Oh, I have no doubt it was not at first in your mind to kill her but…." I shrugged resignedly.

Edwig Crosscastle looked down at his large hands as if they could not possibly be capable of such an atrocity.

"What did you do with her pack?"

Crosscastle, not surprisingly, did not answer.

"Perhaps, when you called in, you'd said that you were just passing and had called to see her. How nice. Putting her at ease, you asked would she like you to take the pack into town for her? I've no doubt she said yes. After you killed her, you dumped it, to lead astray anyone who might investigate her death.

"You got Beecroft to lure the dog away by calling it. He was a good mimic, wasn't he? You knew it would attack you if you approached Elswith."

Crosscastle's eyes narrowed further but he was still silent.

"Then you panicked, for William returned from his journey to fetch blocks from the chalk pit." I chuckled. "I expect you thought he'd gone for the day up to his sheep on the hills.

"There you are with a dead body, pinned in the house. You must have soiled yourself wondering if Will was going to come back into the cottage. Was it always your intention to move Elswith to another house so that William might not be accused of the crime?"

"He loved her. He would never have killed her," said Crosscastle in his deep voice. "I didn't want…."

"But he was taken up for it all the same, wasn't he? All because voices were heard coming from the cottage. You and Elswith arguing. Folk thought it was Will and Elswith."

There was a silence filled only with laughter from one of the guards on the wall walk above our heads.

"How long were you there? It must have been an agonisingly long time for Elswith to begin to stiffen, though the doctor tells me it can be as soon as an hour after death. You must have taken a quick look out in panic, realised William could not see you, fetched the barrow to the door, put the strangely shaped Elswith into it and wheeled it to the next cott. You knew that Floro was out on the downs, you knew that Hilda was at the back of her cottage and could not see up the hill. You dumped the dead woman in Floro's house and fled to your horse, waiting somewhere in the forest."

I yawned. "Oh do forgive me, Crosscastle, I am fatigued with all this...." I sat down at last on the edge of a table opposite Andrew.

"Where was Beecroft all this time, Aumary?" asked Gayle.

"Ah, that was clever. I think he'd secured the dog to the bush and then gone off to retrieve the horse, once Edwig here had ridden as hard as he could for the edge of town. Beecroft then walked the horse back to the castle and Edwig strolled down the High being seen by everyone, including Gilbert Cordwainer."

"An alibi?"

"Of sorts," I said.

"Then Beecroft got too greedy?" asked Andrew.

I nodded. "Not only was he circulating false coin... tut, tut, that wasn't allowed, was it Crosscastle? He also knew that Edwig had killed Elswith. He wanted more money. He had to die."

"So Edwig lured him to the forest and stabbed him, letting the horse do the rest?" said Andrew.

"Yes. And do you know what, Crosscastle? You were seen."

"Never!"

"I chuckled. "Ho, ho, yes you were. By a seven year old girl. My daughter."

"NO! I...."

"She was up in a tree in the forest and she saw you. She found the body of Beecroft. Not a nice thing for a seven year old girl to find. Yes, she saw you. She described you as ugly by the way," I chuckled.

Crosscastle swallowed and looked at his feet.

"Now we come to Carrier. He was responsible for the castle rounceys. He supplied the couriers and messengers coming to and fro. Now you had no accomplice in the stable, because Beecroft was dead, so you had to pretend to be a courier when you wanted to move quickly about the town and the forest. It's easy enough to find an empty pannier with the royal cipher on it here in the castle. Off you went on your borrowed horse and Carrier recognised you. He put two and two together and made... well, fifteen! He knew you'd been a soldier. He knew you could ride. He knew you'd been friendly with Beecroft. He'd seen you skulking about.

"He was going to come and tell me. He was frightened out of his wits that night. You must have overheard him or seen him talking to Chevalier about coming to see me and you knew he had to go."

I mimed a stabbing and a tipping over the wall of the castle.

"Goodbye Carrier."

"No, wait, Aumary!" cried Gayle, putting up both hands. "Edwig was with me. We were out late. There had been a lot of work done. We were coming back from the treasury."

"Here's an example of us taking the word of a trusted man, Pete. Who told you there was a lot of work done? Whose word would you believe when he said why he was still here late?"

Pete's face registered shock and then creased into a frown. "But he was with me when Carrier was up on the wall walk."

"Was he?"

Pete stared at me.

"Was he truly? Had you not sent him to the kitchens for some food?"

"Ah, yes, I had." Pete blinked and shook his head. "But Aumary, he came from the kitchen just as you came down the steps."

"Yes he did, carrying a tray. We all saw him."

"Then how?" asked Pete, rubbing his hands through his white hair.

"If we think about it, it was very dark in the courtyard. The corner by the kitchen is even darker being in shadow. It's not far from there to your office steps. Crosscastle comes quickly down the steps from the wall walk, he passes the kitchen where he has been moments before. We know that trays of food are prepared and left for people. All he had to do was pick one up. He'd previously left the tray on the kitchen step. Then he picks it up and walks into the light where we see him as if he has that moment come from the kitchen."

"But he saw the felon...," began Andrew... and then, as light dawned, "Ah yes, I see now."

"We see what we expect to see, boys. We see a man coming from the direction of the kitchen. We hear him say he has just that moment seen a man running up the keep steps. Who are we to argue?"

"Oh that is...." Pete could not finish.

Crosscastle smiled.

"Then there was me."

"He knew you were getting too close, Aumary" said Andrew.

"He somehow worked out that I'd understood quite a lot of what had been happening. Tostig had to go, of course, because he'd been talking to the ostlers and blacksmiths and Crosscastle couldn't trust them to keep their mouths shut. Just in case Tostig had learned something, he tried to silence him with an arrow in the back. You're a good shot Edwig. Were you a bowman when you were a soldier? I suspect you were."

Again Crosscastle smiled; this time the smile did not travel to his teeth.

"You tried to kill Hal and me on the road from town that evening. How on earth did you survive the dunking in the pool, Edwig? You didn't surface for a very long time. I have to know how you did it?"

The man smirked. "The plants which grow around the edge. Some of them are hollow. You can breathe for a while through them. Not long...but you can do it for a while. I was at the furthest bank and waiting just under the water, until you'd gone," said Crosscastle arrogantly.

"How very clever. You failed to kill me that night but I had to go didn't I?

On the day you tried to kill me FitzAlan had bought some goat's cheese which he intended to eat for his dinner. He tells me he left it in the guard room and when he came to have it, it'd gone."

"Edwig had it?" asked Gayle.

"Yes, and into it he mixed an amount of a rather innocuous substance. Well, it's pretty harmless if you don't eat it, that is."

"Antimony... you told me it was readily available as a cosmetic," said Pete.

"Yes." I turned to Edwig Crosscastle. "Does your wife use such a cosmetic, Edwig?"

Crosscastle scoffed.

"Or perhaps it's here in the workshop? Is antimony used to clean silver perhaps? Is it part of your coin making equipment?"

The man slowly folded his arms over his chest.

"But I didn't die. Hal didn't eat the cheese for he can't abide goat's cheese. The doctor and good Gabriel Gallipot put me back together again and I lived to fight another day."

Crosscastle scoffed again and looked away. This time with a worried expression.

"You must have been hopping mad, Edwig. You must also have been rather afraid. You still didn't know what Tostig had told me did you... if anything."

The man looked up at me with venom in his eyes.

"I nearly had you."

"Yes, you did. The day you came to Johannes' house. I was meant to die then too."

Gayle gasped. "Oh my lord, that was me. I'm so sorry. I told him... he asked me how you were and I said... that you were recovering at the doctor's house. I didn't know."

I squeezed my friend's shoulder. "You weren't to know."

"He went out to market... to fetch us something tasty for our dinner. He wasn't gone long."

"No, he didn't need to be," I said.

I turned back to Crosscastle. "You weren't as busy as you made out, were you, moneyer. You told me and others that you were busy in your forge from just after dawn to dusk but you could come and go at will. No one would notice and no one would argue if you went missing."

"Another example of us believing what he said," said Andrew.

"A trustworthy man, why would he lie to us? We didn't check. Why should we?"

I sighed. "What I really don't understand is the involvement of my cow keeper, Kineman."

Both Andrew and Gayle sat up at that. "Who, Aumary?" stammered Gayle.

"I had a serf. He lived at Braydon and was a cowman. He looked to my cattle pastured at Braydon Meadow. The night before last my daughter Hawise saw him talking to Crosscastle there in my own stables."

Crosscastle's head came up. "I've never been to Durley."

"My daughter and, by the way, Tostig, saw you."

I heard him mumble under his breath "Not her again."

"Yes, her again. She recognised you as the man she saw in the forest and listened carefully. She is only seven but she managed to remember and to tell me what she heard. She didn't understand it all. I don't understand it all. I cannot, cannot see my cowman being involved in your metal stealing for he never came into town. It seems you asked Kineman to kill Tostig."

Crossman chuckled under his breath. "The word of a seven year old girl! Pah!"

"Why would you do that? You normally did your own killing, Edwig"

"Because I didn't. That's why."

"Well, whatever happened, poor Kineman was killed that night."

"It wasn't me."

"You rode leisurely for the church at Cadley. Incidentally, I'm told that's where you were born and brought up."

"Cadley's the arse end of the forest but it's no crime to be born there."

I chuckled quietly, "You know every inch of the place, don't you?"

Crosscastle shrugged.

"Tostig followed as you'd hoped he would."

The moneyer laughed out loud. "Bloody fool. Did he really think I didn't know he was there behind me the whole time?"

"Again you were seen."

"Don't tell me... your daughter?"

"No, a ten year old boy called Nod."

"Bloody brats."

"You imprisoned Tostig in the secret space under Cadley church, hoping to come back and find out from him what he'd told me. If I knew all about you... were you going to flee or would you brave it out as you are doing now?"

The moneyer shrugged again, "He's dead... the church burned down. He'll tell you nothing now."

"Too late moneyer; Tostig is as safe as a mouse in a malt heap. Alive and back home."

At that, I saw his jaw tense and he ground his teeth.

"So you left him, rode back to work and would come back later to get the truth from him. You rode your rouncey to the limit and surprised Kineman as he entered his home. He wouldn't do as you asked."

Crosscastle gave a low chuckle.

"He was another cousin you know. Ha! I see you didn't. Yes, Thomas was another member of our huge family. He too was born in Cadley, except he was the unfree part of the family. A villein, whereas my father... well anyway, he was very fond of cousin Elswith and when she died, I played on that. I told him that it was Tostig who had killed her."

"Ah...."

"Stupid bastard believed me."

"We all believed you, Edwig," said Gayle crossly.

"I was trying to get him to avenge her, kill Tostig... he was nearly there... when who should turn up but the bastard himself. Kineman got cold feet and fled. I just knew the stupid idiot would go to the authorities, so yes, I killed him."

"And then you raced back to find that the church had burnt down. Good, you thought - you hoped as you trotted home, Tostig gone without speaking to me."

"Shame about the church. It was quite a nice building."

"Incidentally, Crosscastle, out of interest, what is that place underneath it? It's not part of the original church. Father Justin knew nothing about it."

"I discovered it when I was a lad, roaming about the woods. It's very old... great place to hide out... I'll show you... wait."

Crosscastle stood and lifted his hands. "No... no weapon... see... I'll just step over there and get it... it's just there, this thing."

I stood up ready to intervene. Stephen lifted his back from the wall where he'd been leaning. Andrew shifted on his table. Gayle leaned forward and watched Crosscastle as he walked slowly to the garderobe. I watched carefully, making for the door space.

"What can you possibly have hidden here? The room is locked... come away."

Peter Devizes had checked the whole room for weapons before we had begun. We knew he could have no knife or anything secreted there.

We waited a heartbeat.

Then there was a wooden scuffling and a whooshing sound followed by a dull thud.

Being the closest, I ran into the latrine.

Crosscastle was gone.

He had slipped down the garderobe chute.

Chapter Fourteen

We lurched for the door and ran down the dark passageway of the castle entrance. I was the last from the room and I heard, coming from the base of the latrine, a sharp cry, a shouting and then a gurgling. I didn't stop to investigate.

Andrew grabbed a torch from a startled gate guard and we raced for the wicket in the main gate, ducking under the half lowered portcullis.

Stephen had rounded the end of the tower by the time I'd got onto the grass at the base of the castle.

I could hear more shouting. I stopped to listen.

"Hal?" I yelled as I ran on.

Peter, who had been ahead of us, had stopped at the corner of the tower. Suddenly he burst out laughing.

I joined him on the grass. Andrew had lifted his torch and the yellow glow picked out my chief man at arms, Hal of Potterne, one arm around Crosscastle's body and the other pushing the man's head into the pile of ordure which had collected at the base of the garderobe chute.

He pulled the man up by his hair, shifted him slightly and dunked him in the water of the moat.

I heard him growl. "And that's for tryin' it on with Tostig as well!"

Presumably, the ordure was for the attempt on my life.

"Hal!" I laughed. "Let the man up, you're drowning him." I shook with laughter.

"I never disobey an order, sir... but... this one I am going not to 'ear for another 'eartbeat or two."

Eventually, Crosscastle came up spluttering and cursing.

Peter took him from Hal, and raised him up. Holding him at arm's length, he wrinkled his nose.

Stephen proffered a hand to Hal. He jumped up and promptly kicked the man hard on the shins.

"And that's for my lovely blue tunic, you barbarian."

"What are you doing here, man?" I said, coming closer. Hal smoothed down his beard and adjusted his tunic, which tonight was sea green, though it was grey in the meagre light.

"Well, it's like this, lad."

Crosscastle heaved and coughed, spat and retched.

"When you told me what you was a goin' a do, I 'ad a thought to come to the castle and see if I could get in. I shouted to be let in and the guards let me in but you weren't at the forge. I thought then you might all be in the guardroom. But no. No one seemed to know where you were. Your office was locked. So I thought that I'd come out 'ere' an listen at the base of the tower. I walked round a bit and found I could hear through the window. I wanted to know what was goin' on. I could just 'ear, see, through de Devil's room's window." This was Hal's personal name for my superior.

"I'm very glad you did Hal."

"Well, you can imagine what a shock this piece o' piss, forgive me m'lord, gave me, when he comes sliding down that shit chute an' nearly knocked me into the moat."

Stephen guffawed. I stifled a laugh.

"C'mon, let's get him into the castle and to the gaol. We'll let him stew in... his own and others' juices for a while" I chuckled.

We all trooped back to the safety of the castle wall and Andrew and Gayle took the surly Crosscastle up to the gaol at the base of the keep.

I shouted after them "Gyves and manacles Pete! We don't want him making another bid for freedom."

"Pergh!" said Andrew Merriman. "He stinks like a midden. I'll leave that to you, Pete."

It was warm in Andrew's guardroom; there was a real wintery chill blowing from the north and we all crowded round the lit brazier as we waited for Pete and Andrew to return.

Stephen rubbed his hands together. "That's him for the hempen necklace then, sir?"

"Yes, Stephen. Thank you for your help. You too, Peter."

We began to thaw out and I looked round for some ale which someone usually brought into the guardroom for the guards to drink in the night.

"Have we anything to warm this up?"

"My knife's just cleaned sir, we could use that if you want," said Peter Devizes. He thrust it into the brazier and took hold of a cloth, ready to lift it out and plunge it into our mugs.

We all watched the brazier flaring into life as Stephen took the small bellows to it.

The gate guards, Hardcastle and Castleman, Felix the cordwainer's apprentice's father, sat at the back and made themselves comfortable on their usual benches. Hardiman, the third guard was outside on watch for a while.

We chatted desultorily as the wind whistled around the bailey and buffeted one or two shutters.

After a while, I began to be worried. "They should be back by now," I said.

"Nah… don't you worry," said Hal, "All the fight went outta 'im when he landed in that pile o' sh…."

"What's bin goin' on, sir?" said Hardcastle with a perplexed frown. "What's Master Crosscastle done?"

So I started to tell them the story. After a short while we heard a horse coming into the gateway. A voice challenged. Another answered.

"King's courier," said Castleman. "Came in just as it was going dark. I reckon he's had summat to eat and then saddled up a new horse and he's off to… wherever he's going."

"All hours o' the day and night," added Hardcastle. "Jesus, I don't know how they do it."

I smiled. The gate guard outside opened the gate and raised the portcullis and I heard the horse clatter over the bridge.

I was still feeling uncomfortable.

"Hal, come with me quick."

Stephen and Peter followed us out. We ran across the bailey and up the keep steps, my heart thumping with more than the rapid climb up thirty or more steps.

I ducked down into the gaol which lay under the keep at the top of the mound.

Gayle's keys were in the lock. The room had been locked from the outside. I turned it.

I'd heard Andrew hammering and yelling as I approached the door. I pulled it back.

Andrew fell out, his head dripping blood.

"He's bolted. Attacked Gayle before we could get the gyves on him." He ran past me and made for the keep steps. "Hit me with Gayle's knife handle."

I looked into the gloom of the gaol floor. Pete lay sprawled on his back, moaning. Hal went to see to him. "Hal, fetch Johannes," I said.

"Right you are, sir."

I turned back down the steps. "Andrew... he's got a horse and is out of the castle. He's posed as a courier again."

I saw Andrew swerve and run in the direction of the stable.

Agonising moments later we were saddled and racing for the gateway ourselves.

"Which way?" asked Stephen, hesitating on the road into town.

I bit my lip. "Look, there's the watch, let's ask..." We cantered into the middle of the High Street.

The two watchmen who patrolled the town at night, hoping to keep the curfew and law and order in the dark, saw us approaching. I shouted my name long before we reached them.

"A courier on a brown rouncey?"

"Out by Oxford Street sir. A few moments ago."

"He's making for the forest, I bet," said Andrew.

"He knows the nearer forest quite well. But not quite as well as I do," I smiled.

We raced up the hill at a furious pace, irrespective of the potholes and pitfalls which could waylay us on the uneven road.

Once we stopped, close by Walter's Pit, to listen. Sure enough there ahead of us on the chalk road was a hard ridden horse. We spurred our mounts on.

We reached Cadley village and stopped. The air was still filled with the smell of the smoke of the burned church and we heard no hoofbeats echoing down the deserted road.

"NO! He can't have gone to ground here," I spat. "His hiding place is compromised."

"Unless he has another," said Andrew.

Stephen found the rouncey a couple of moments later. The horse was shivering and breathing hard. Its eyes were wild. It tossed its head as we approached.

These horses were fearless creatures, able to run for hours but they weren't fast. This one had been driven to the limit up and down steep hills.

I patted his foam flecked neck as I passed. "We shall get you home soon," I said.

I loosened my knife and my sword.

"Crosscastle was born here. I wonder if there's still a family home?"

Andrew shrugged. "We can ask."

"Aye we'll knock up the Harts. They're the nearest."

It was some time before my forester answered the door.

"Who wants me... what time is this to come....?" He shouted through the door.

"Osmund; it's Lord Belvoir. Let me in."

I heard the bolt slide back.

"M'lord, whatever is…"

"Crosscastle, Hart. Where's his family home? Are his parents still here?"

Hart looked startled. "No sir, both died in the dock fever we had a while back."

"The cottage?"

"The first one in the trees, back of the church sir. North of it."

"Lived in now?" I really ought to have known this but I left such details to my reeves and other officers. I couldn't know and do everything. Savernake was a huge place.

"No sir. Empty and falling down."

"Thank you. Stay here and bolt the doors."

Hart slowly shut the door with the most puzzled expression on his face. I saw his wife Godgifu frowning behind him. Then the light from his candle disappeared.

"Back some way - over there," I said, as I joined Stephen and Andrew by our horses. "We go on foot I think."

As quietly as we could we made our way across the ground at the northern side of the small churchyard.

The bracken and docks, willowherb and grasses had died down. However they weren't as dry they might have been for we'd had rain recently. They didn't betray our steps with a crispy sound as we travelled through them.

I took out my sword as quietly as I could.

There was no light in the cottage, the usual one up and one down affair. The thatch had slid down into the house place and the right hand side of the cottage was open to the elements with half a wall. The left hand side was still quite well thatched and the door which lay in this half was open and serviceable.

We stopped and listened. As we did the moon came out obligingly from behind the scudding clouds, lighting up the cottage and showing us Crosscastle, searching frantically, shifting old furniture and items in the habitable part of the dwelling. He didn't seem to mind how much noise he made. He was counting on us not following so readily.

I filled my lungs with smoke tinged air. "Crosscastle!" I yelled. "Give up now. We have you. You cannot hope to escape."

The man swung round with a sack in his hand and swore. He leapt for a small trestle just visible through the doorway and pushed it onto its side and blocked the hole. He hunkered down behind it.

In the next heartbeat, an arrow came thudding into the tree nearest to me.

I caught Andrew's eye. He gestured that he would try to work his way round the cottage.

I nodded. I would need to keep the forgemaster busy.

"So, Crosscastle. You were about to tell me what the place under the church is."

A deep chuckle came from behind the planking of the table.

"I told you it was very old."

"Yes."

"What's the oldest people you know of who inhabited the forest?" I could hear him scurrying around on his hands and knees in the small space of the house. He had, I suspected, had stuff concealed here should he need to flee.

"C'mon Edwig, both you and I know that there are many tumps, earthworks and barrows here in the forest. They are the oldest, I'm told. This is a much more sophisticated type of building."

I craned my neck to see if I could see Andrew. Another arrow came whistling in my direction.

"There's a bloody great road going right through the middle of Savernake," shouted the moneyer.

"Aye. You can see it here and there. Still walk the paving blocks."

"Romans, Belvoir. Romans."

Stephen came up behind me. "Sir Andrew's just about at the side wall now, sir," he whispered.

"Ah yes, the road comes from Mildenhall, once called Cunetio, across the river and up the slope," I shouted.

"Major route it was," answered Crosscastle. I saw him rise slightly and stare at the right hand wall of the cott.

"Can you get him, Stephen, with your knife?"

Stephen shook his head. "No, sir too far away."

"Damn."

"Tell your man to back off, Belvoir. I shall skewer him the moment he's visible. I have a spear in here trained on the wall."

"You've got yourself a nice little pile of weapons there I see, moneyer."

"Ready for anything," said Crosscastle. "A soldier has to be on his guard and ready for anything," he chuckled.

Suddenly I heard a snapping sound. Andrew had trodden on a branch. I saw Crossscastle whip round and let an arrow loose into the hole where the wall used to be.

"Back off I say."

"Andrew...?"

"Aye, I heard."

The moon was now quite bright and lit up the small glade in which the cottage lay. I shifted to a nearer tree. Yet another arrow came my way.

"Got enough arrows have you, Crosscastle?" I chuckled.

"Enough for my purpose."

There was a wooden scraping sound from inside the cottage.

Stephen scurried up beside me and fell to his knees leaning on the tree trunk. "Want me to get behind the cottage, sir? Maybe two of us...."

I looked up at the moon.

"The moon's our friend Stephen, but also our foe. We can see him but he can see us too."

He nodded. "What are we to do then, sir?"

I looked up at the moon again. "We wait. I think he'll get a little impatient soon and maybe make a move."

We waited in silence. No more sound came from the cottage. A tawny owl hooted, cross at being disturbed in his hunting.

Small things, the prey of the owl, scurried about in the undergrowth.

"Crosscastle!" I yelled. "You realise that with the dawn the place will be crawling with my men from the castle. Best you give up now."

There was no answer. No movement. No arrow. "You'll certainly die."

My voice died away in the cold air.

"Andrew!" I yelled.

"Aumary... he's gone, I think. There's no noise from inside."

"No! Where? Where's he gone?"

Stephen and I bent double and ran for the cottage, flattening ourselves by the wall. A moment later Andrew joined us. No arrow came at us from inside.

Stephen took out his sword and leapt into the cottage, over the face of the toppled trestle.

Andrew followed.

"Nothing. Gone."

I kicked the plank in frustration. It shifted.

"Jesus!" said Stephen, crossing himself. "Has he been raiding our armoury?"

We noticed a spear or two propped up by the door and one angled up to the side wall where Andrew had recently hidden. It was lodged in between a chest and some debris of stones.

There was a box of arrows: only three remained. A discarded bow lay behind the table. A sword lay flat on the beaten earth floor.

"I can't think he's gone without weapons, Stephen." I said. "I suspect he has as many with him as he's left here."

"Aumary!" hissed Andrew. "Look."

At the very back of the cottage, beneath a crude chest pushed aside, was a hole with a wooden lid. I used my strike-a-light to ignite a piece of cloth from the floor and I offered it to the space. The lid was open. There were steep steps going down into the ground.

"Find some light and follow me, both of you." I turned sideways and moved carefully onto the first step, throwing away the tinder cloth after lighting a stub of a candle from my purse. There were twelve steps, just as there had been to the underground passageway which John Brenthall and I had discovered.

Cautiously, I worked my way to the bottom and listened.

Here too there was a finely made floor of paved stones exactly fitted together. In the middle here I saw a man with a bull.

I crawled along it at a snail's pace, watching carefully for side passages or secret alcoves where a man might hide. There was nothing.

Eventually after about twelve feet it widened into an oblong space about three yards by six. By the light of my meagre candle, I could see that a stone lintel framed what would have been a door if the wood had survived.

I gripped my sword firmly and stepped through the space.

The room had the same type of floor as the space at the end of the passageway leading under the church. I saw more of the panels of small blocks of stone made into patterns. Some were missing here but it was possible to see what the pictures represented. I'd seen something similar at Gallipot's workshop, in a book.

Each square, two blocks wide and six deep had an astrological sign in it. I lifted my candle. I recognised the ram, my own sign and that of the half man, half horse with his bow nocked, Lydia's birth sign. My candle guttered and then I was plunged into darkness.

I made for the wall and put my back to it. Stephen and Andrew would be here in a moment with some more light.

"Crosscastle." I whispered.

The man laughed a deep throaty and hideous laugh. The sort that Hawise must have heard him make in the forest the day Beecroft died. From what I could tell, the man was at the furthest end of the space.

"Welcome to the narthex, Sir Aumary," he chuckled.

"What's that, moneyer?"

He chuckled again. "You don't know? This is the outer chamber of the temple. The bigger room under the church was the temple itself."

"Ah...."

The moneyer struck a light. He placed a lit candle onto a stone shelf about four feet from the ground, all the while keeping his eyes on me. He lit another and another. The stone wall grew around me.

I marvelled at the complexity of it. The floor was now completely visible.

"The twelve astrological signs," said the moneyer, picking up his bow and loading it with an arrow.

"I'm Sagitttarius. The bowman."

"You'd have to be wouldn't you?" I mocked.

I heard Andrew and Stephen coming down the passage. "Be careful!" I shouted. "He has a bow."

The footsteps slowed.

Crosscastle wore a belt into which was thrust a knife. A sword in a plain scabbard lay at his hip. No doubt he had, as had I, a further knife at his hip behind him and if he was as crafty as myself, another small one secreted in his boot.

He aimed the arrow at me.

"The passageway you discovered, Sir Aumary, is of no real importance and was just a service corridor."

"Still so beautifully decorated?"

"Yes. They decorated everything, these peoples. This is the place where the supplicants would gather to be cleansed and purified before the ritual. That takes place in there...."

He nodded over his shoulder. "Though now of course, it's full of charred church timbers."

"Who was the God?"

"Mithras. The Bull Slayer."

"How do you know so much about it?"

"My soldiering days weren't just made up of killing and looting, you know," he said, sarcasm in his tone. "I learned a few things."

"Haha, that's what my friend the doctor says. He travelled with King Richard to the Holy land."

"I got as far as Malta."

"And there…?"

"Yes, there I learned what there was to know about the worship of Mithras. There were several temples on the island, all visible. Of course I'd known this place since a child. My father discovered the hole under the house, when part of it caved in and our floor disappeared. I knew about the other end."

"Stonefalls have closed it off, haven't they?"

"In parts. It's possible to get into the main temple; well, it was until it burned."

"I was wrong about the moneying, wasn't I?"

Crosscastle laughed.

"Stupid ol' Beecroft. I allowed him to play around with coins. He and I made a few at his house... just to make him think he was clever and useful."

"But here was where you did the work in earnest. Good coins. Better coins. Coins with much less silver in them."

Crosscastle nodded. "Here I could melt the silver again. Here it was safe and silent."

"With just your Roman ghosts for company."

Crosscastle reached for a sack at his feet. He tossed it onto Gemini, the twins.

"I defy you to tell the difference between those and the coins which I minted every day under the watchful eyes of Gayle. But of course, they are half copper."

I stepped away from the wall. "So what now, Crosscastle?"

"I leave... and you...." he aimed carefully at my breast. "Die."

The arrow left the bow. Suddenly out of the space at my back came a throwing knife. Crosscastle's bow was knocked awry by the accurate throw. Stephen... I knew he was good knifeman.

I leapt forward and sideways, dodging the now impotent arrow.

Crosscastle dropped the bow and pulled the sword from his scabbard in a fluid movement. At the same moment, Andrew and Stephen stepped in through the doorway.

"NO!" I cried as I saw Andrew about to leap forward. "He's mine."

"Aumary!"

"No. He's killed two of my people. He's nearly killed Tostig - twice - and he's almost killed me, not to mention frightening my daughter to death. He's mine, Andrew."

I saw Andrew shrug. "If he kills you, Aumary... what do I tell Lydia?"

"That you killed my killer! I cried and leapt for the middle of the room.

*****

I landed on the scales, Libra. The moneyer came up and took guard before me. He stood on Capricorn the goat. Andrew moved a little way to the side and stood opposite Aquarius the water bearer. Stephen made his way to stand opposite the crab, Cancer; both leaned against the wall.

"Like a game of chess, isn't it?" chuckled Crosscastle as he threw away his long robe to free him up to fight.

He jumped one panel closer and kicked the bag of coins out of the way.

"First move." He landed on Aquarius. "Your move."

I backed onto Cancer.

He chuckled and moved forward to take a swipe at my head. I took one hand from my pommel, parried with my right hand and with my left took hold of the blade in my gloved hand. Up came my sword, I twisted and turned the moneyer's blade and then with my free arm pinned him by the neck. He jumped back just in time for me to miss disarming him.

A two handed swipe then followed and I backed out of his way, tilted my sword down and came at him with the point. I just missed his midriff. He jumped back onto Capricorn.

Two strikes later and my sword's edge caught his blade and pushed it down. A swift upward movement to the left allowed me to get my blade to his unprotected side. He rolled his body out of the way very quickly.

I advanced to Gemini. Crosscastle came at me with a powerful downward strike. I parried his strike and again my gloved hand grasped my own blade and I used it as a club, turning the pommel into his face. I caught his cheek bone and heard it crack.

He backed off with a cry, blinking and circled me to stand on Taurus. I left him a moment to recover before I made for him with a left handed swipe. He'd half turned and I was able to get under his guard, turn his sword over his head and come at him from underneath. I would've had him in the ribs then, but he spat in my eye and I had to retreat to Sagittarius.

"Crosscastle, you should've stuck to your bow. You had much more success with it," I laughed.

The man danced away on light feet. He too turned his sword and the razor sharp cross piece came for my eyes. Weighted as it was, it was too slow and too heavy a blow and missed me to fall harmlessly to my right hand side. Crosscastle recovered and moved diagonally forward to Gemini.

"Never learned the sword properly did we, moneyer?" mocked Andrew, circling us.

The technique of using both hands was something which Hal had discovered when he'd been a younger man on his travels in France and he'd passed the skill on to me.

I strode forward and struck at him again. The moneyer parried.

"C'mon Luke!" shouted Andrew. "Aumary is playing with you. You can't hope to beat him."

"He's kept up his swordplay, I'll give him that, Andrew," I exclaimed. "I didn't think he'd get this far."

Right handed I went for the moneyer and feinted a strike to the neck. His sword came up to meet mine. Half way down I turned the blade crossways on his, stepped forward, simultaneously pushed down and forward and caught him a blow in the chest with my point. His blade ineffectually pointed down.

He stepped back quickly, hissing.

"Crosscastle, you are not my match. Give in now."

"Just because you're a knight and I'm a foot soldier, eh?"

He lunged at me angrily and gave a series of blows which I took on the blade without answering. He'd advanced to Libra. I shifted diagonally to Aquarius.

Dancing on the balls of my feet I came forward.

I gave a blow to his sword which came up to meet mine, transferred my grip to my left hand, twisted upwards, pulled his blade down with my own until his point hit the floor and grabbed his wrist.

He struggled. The point of my own sword was inches from his neck.

Crosscastle ducked down, dropped his sword and fled through the door hole at his back. I staggered forward with the momentum of the blow.

I threw my sword to Andrew and grabbed the knife from my hip, pursuing Crosscastle into the body of the ruined temple underneath the church

The moon lit the fallen charred roof beams and stone from the floor of the building. Very little could be seen of the temple beneath them. It was a mass of cracked flagstones, burnt wood and charred plaster.

I scanned the space. There, outlined in the moonlight, was the figure of a man gingerly climbing up on one of the fallen beams to the ground above. The altar at the eastern end of the church had fallen in one lump and now stood at a jaunty angle in the temple, covered with beams. Smoke still swirled around some areas.

The moneyer reached and clambered up the crossing beams which littered the temple floor, giving himself a leg up onto the altar. Zigzagging from one to the other he slithered along, missing his footing here and there and clinging on, hauling himself up. Some of the beams partly disintegrated as he stepped on them.

He looked back once.

I followed. He was much a slighter man than I and my weight more than once made the crisscrossing beams give way. I hung on and swung myself up on to the altar. I gave a 'sorry' to God and struggled upright.

I screamed at Andrew and Stephen. "Go back the other way. Head him off!"

Crosscastle had climbed the twelve feet or so up to the ground level and was clambering over the stone plinth of the old church.

I struggled on, putting out my hands for balance. I looked up. He'd gone.

I slipped from a beam and grabbed for the nearest handhold. It came away in my hand, nothing but a bundle of twigs and charred thatch.

I hung on by one hand. Gradually I swung myself up and managed to get one foot over the edge of the plinth. Bending backwards like a bow, I eased myself over the edge, testing my poor, still sore, stomach muscles to their limit. I knew I was vulnerable to a blow now, but what else could I do?

No blow came. I saw Crosscastle running back to the road and to the place where he'd left his horse.

Footsteps were thumping up to my right, "He's back to his horse," cried Andrew.

"Damn!"

We ran across the grass, leaping the humped graves and small bushes littering the ground.

As we approached the path to the road, we heard the rouncey whinny.

Suddenly from the darkness on my left came another figure running along the road. I didn't stop to see who it was but plunged on regardless.

There was another whinny and a cry. Then we heard the sound of the rouncey's hooves hitting the ground. It didn't move far.

A peal of childish laughter rang out.

I stopped at the end of the path. The castle rouncey had run on several yards. Out of the undergrowth came Nod and grabbed her reins and spoke sweetly into her ear.

I looked across to where we'd tethered the rouncey. Crosscastle was getting up from the surface of the road. The saddle was lying beside him.

"Well done, Nod!" I shouted. "Well done!"

I vaulted the small gate which passed as the entrance to the churchyard and advanced on the moneyer.

He shook his head, looked up the road at the horse, ahead at me, down the road at the soldiers advancing on him and ran into the undergrowth behind him.

"You can't escape, Crosscastle. I'll have my men in every inch of the forest tomorrow. They'll find you," I yelled, with the rest of the breath in me.

Stephen and Andrew came up to me also out of breath.

"Where did he go?"

I gestured. "We'll follow. He's probably heading for Kingstones."

I looked past the two soldiers down the road towards Marlborough. A few village folk had come out of their houses to gawp at the people making all the noise in the middle of the night, in their quiet little village.

"This is the Lord Belvoir," I cried. "Go home and lock your doors."

People turned back muttering, disappointed that the action was not going to include them.

"Thank you Andrew," I said, taking hold of my weapon again.

As I thrust my sword back into my scabbard I saw a movement back along the road towards Marlborough. Our felon had appeared again, silhouetted in the moonlight. He looked back once. The figure of Hal, my chief man at arms, appeared at the edge of the forest and made for the moneyer, sword drawn.

"Hal!"

Hal looked neither right nor left but continued to pursue Crosscastle, who now fled again to the greenery on the church side of the road. They both disappeared into the trees. I swear I heard Hal say, "I can't 'ear you m'lord."

"Where the Hell is he going, sir?" asked Stephen.

"Looks like Hal headed him off and he's doubled back. Perhaps he's for the cottage again. He's still got weapons there."

We turned about and once more vaulted the gate of the churchyard.

We slowed as we approached the small cottage which had belonged to Crosscastle's family.

The moneyer was running towards it and Hal was gaining.

"Hal!" I yelled, "leave him… he has weapons there."

We resumed our pounding across the grass and came up to the side of the house which had fallen in. Feet ahead of us Crosscastle was perched on the flimsy remnants of the wall, facing out, six feet above his attacker. He parried a knife sweep from Hal of Potterne's long dagger. He kicked out. Hal dodged.

Hal went for the man's legs.

Crosscastle teetered on the six foot wall. Some thatch slipped down from above him. A few stones dislodged.

The man began to fall back, flailing his arms.

I reached Hal just as he stretched out his hand and gently pushed the unsteady Crosscastle from his perch. Hal was grinning, I noticed.

Crosscastle fell with an oomph.

Then there was a hideous cry.

I levered myself up beside Hal on tiptoe onto the remains of the wall and peered over into the body of the house.

Crosscastle struggled, screaming as the head of the spear he'd placed there a while before to deter Andrew, slowly pierced him from the groin up. He tried to lift himself from it. The haft was wedged fast in the debris of the cott. Then his falling weight moved it. It slid inexorably into him and as the haft shifted, the blade scored a line along his torso and deep into it.

Crosscastle convulsed. He screamed while there was breath in him. Hal peered over the wall.

The moneyer's eyes bulged and his lips drew back in a hideous grimace showing his perfect white teeth. Then his mouth filled with blood.

"Checkmate, I think," I said, as the man died.

*****

Hal dropped from the wall and slid down the outside, his back to the stones. I sat down by him, my knees raised.

"I'm getting too old for all this runnin' about," he said, his sides heaving.

"How did you...?"

Stephen and Andrew now came up to the house and Andrew peered in the door.

Stephen kicked the trestle away and went to check on Crosscastle.

"I saw the watch. They told me you'd gone up the 'ill. I came across Nod and 'e said 'e'd seen you. I ran into the churchyard and then I 'eard yer. The bastard came running past me and I missed 'im by a wrinkle. So I chased him in the forest and headed him off."

"Well done, old friend," I said. "Well done. What would we have done without you this night?"

I looked him in the eye. "How is Gayle?" My heart was in my mouth.

"Sliced but only a flesh wound," said Hal.

Stephen came around the edge of the cottage. "Spitted like a boar for the roastin' he was, sir."

Andrew followed, wiping his forehead on his sleeve. He leaned against the wall.

"Jesu!" he said, "what a way to go?"

Hal beamed up at the captain of the guard, "Good wunnit? Nearly sliced in two. Slowly. No more than the bugger deserved."

I chuckled at my man at arms. He could be so wonderfully gentle and yet, as he had proved tonight, he could also be as vengeful as a thwarted devil.

We couldn't get the spear from Crosscastle's body and so someone borrowed an axe and we chopped it short.

We slung him over the horse and gathered up our own beasts.

Nod came shyly up to me, holding the saddle which the rouncey had worn.

He could just hold it up, he was so small and skinny.

"Nah lad. You keep it. It's yours now. If anyone says you didn't catch a vicious murderer, you show them that."

The boy beamed. "Thanks sir." He put it at his feet. "But I don't think me da will let me keep it."

"We'll see," I said. "That was very clever of you to cut the saddle straps so as the man tried to ride away, he'd fall off."

"I thought it might help you save some time, sir, and keep him back. He weren't so quick without Ol' Agilis."

"You know the horse?"

"A corse I do, sir." Nod looked past me at the darkness surrounding the body on the horse, with Stephen at its head.

"Is he really dead, sir?"

"As dead as last summer, Nod."

"Cor."

An agonised voice rang out around the space in which we stood. "Nod! Aelfnod where are you?" It was a worried voice but also a little angry.

"Here!" I shouted and put my arm around the small boy.

Aelfnod's mother came into view, her hair flying free, her cloak wrapped around her. She saw me and stopped. Osmund came up behind her, carrying a hayfork.

"You'll not be needing that, Osmund," I said. "And you should be very proud of your lad."

"You were told to stay in and you...."

"But mam...."

I put up my hand. "No Godgifu, he's not to be admonished. He's done us a good turn tonight. We have Elswith Larkworthy's killer because of him."

"The master says I can have the fella's saddle to remind me," said Nod proudly.

"You.... No, no you can't...."

"No arguments," I said.

Osmund came forward and grabbed Nod by the shoulder. "We were frightened to death at where you'd gone."

"I was only on the road, da."

"You should've been in your bed."

Nod hung his head.

"No, Nod, they aren't really angry, believe me," I said, "They are just relieved you are all right. I do this too, to my little girl. I get all cross and then I realise I'm cross because really I've been so worried and the relief makes me short tempered."

I heard Hal guffaw behind me. Osmund blinked.

"It's late. Let's all go home and get some rest, eh?"

Nod turned to go home with his parents. Godgifu curtsied. I nodded to the saddle. Osmund picked it up with a sigh and tucked it under his arm.

"Nod!"

"Yessir?"

"How old are you?"

"I shall be twelve tomorrow, sir."

"Aye" said his mother breathily, ruffling his hair, "You shall."

And I had thought him much younger because he was so small.

"Then Happy Birthday, for I do think that we are past the midnight hour."

The lad grinned.

"Nod, do you still want to be a groom?"

"Oh yes, sir. More than anything."

"Then Osmund, bring him on Tuesday to Durley. We'll introduce him to my stables and to the folk that work there. Anson, my youngest groom, will be fourteen soon and he'll be moving from his parents' house in Durley village to the stable loft. He could do with a stable mate."

Nod's face was a picture of joy and he would have embraced me if he'd been allowed.

As it was his mother hugged her eldest offspring tightly to her side and thanked me. But as she looked up at me, there were tears in her eyes.

Chapter Fifteen

Wearily we trotted back to the castle. Stephen and Peter borrowed Gayle's keys and unlocked the gaol. They dumped the body of Edwig Crosscastle in the smallest cell and locked the door again.

Johannes and Gayle were in Pete's room and Gayle was sitting on his bed with his ribs bandaged. Johannes was helping him on with a clean tunic, when we all squeezed in through the door.

"You got him?" grimaced Peterkin.

"Aye, dead."

"Ah well. It saves us the cost of having to feed him whilst we wait for the justices," he said. "And saves the cost of a hanging."

Johannes put a mug of something in his hands.

"Drink, Pete. It will help with the pain."

Andrew threw himself on Pete's chair and lolled there, totally spent.

"I know what you're doing," said Gayle. "Don't think I don't. I'll not drink until you've told me every gory detail. I shan't sleep until you've finished your tale."

I chuckled. "All right then," and began the story at the point where he and Andrew had left us.

"What happened in the gaol?"

"The man was like a wet willow strand. Dragging his feet, falling over, bending like a sapling in a storm. We thought him a spent force."

"Took two of us, Aumary, to hold him up," said Andrew Merriman.

"Of course it was all bluff. He was no more finished than a flan," said Gayle, smiling.

"We got into the small cell. I'd got the keys to the gyves. I turned to lift the manacles from the wall and Crosscastle suddenly came alive and grabbed my knife from its scabbard at my hip."

"It's bloody dark in that gaol at night," said Andrew, yawning. "I'd turned to catch up a lantern from the outside wall to light it, so Pete could see to lock the man up."

"Next we knew, he'd sliced me in the ribs and gave Andrew a hefty whack on the head with the hilt, leapt out of the door and locked it," said Pete.

"The rest you know," said Andrew.

Between us we managed to tell Pete how we'd cornered Crosscastle and how he'd died.

He shook his head. "The man had us all so fooled, even to the end. We all underestimated him in the extreme. He seemed so mild."

I yawned. "He was a hard fighting man masquerading as a soft artisan."

"'E 'ad a 'ard death," said Hal, folding his arms tightly. " 'E's rotting in 'ell."

"I've known him oh... it must be eight years, maybe. Never an inkling of the 'other' Crosscastle... this Luke... which I suppose you're right, was his name for money, lucrum... profit, money."

"No, like you say he had us all fooled."

"Never again will I accept what someone says," said Pete, shaking his head. "Never."

"Aw c'mon Pete," said Hal. "None of us can live like that. We all 'ave to trust someone and like you say, you knew 'im eight years."

"Just goes to show you, that you can't really know a person," said Andrew, peeling back the sticky hair from his head wound with a grimace.

Johannes looked across at him. "Let me see that, Andrew."

"Nah... it's just a graze and a bruise."

Johannes lifted Andrew's chin. "I'll clean it up."

"It's nothing."

"Many a man's said that and died a few days later of poisoning."

Andrew chuckled and let the doctor bathe the wound.

"I suppose I'll have to go round tomorrow and tell the widow...." I rubbed my forehead where a headache was beginning. "God... how am I going to explain..."

"The truth, Aumary... there's nothing you can tell but the truth," said Johannes.

"That she is no longer a contender for the Flitch contest," said Hal cruelly.

We all looked at him in silence.

"What?" he said, offended. "It's true. Not a word of a lie."

"Aye... it's true," I said at last, giving a suppressed chuckle.

Johannes turned from ministering to Andrew. "Do you want me to tell her? I'm used to giving folk bad news."

I nodded gratefully.

Andrew struggled up from his chair. "I'm off to my bed...."

"You sit back down, sir," said Johannes sternly, with a pot in his hand. "I'm not finished with you yet. I have a salve for that head of yours."

*****

A few days later I was back alone up on the downs where all this had begun. On a frosty late February morning, I sat on Bayard looking out over the hills dotted with white sheep.

This time my young wolfhound Mildred was with me. She sat and thumped her tail on the rabbit cropped grass, scanning the flocks with disinterested eyes.

How different I thought, was this dog from my gazehound, Holdfast, who would've been off at the least movement. To her, the chase was everything. Mildred was a sitter and thinker. When she was just a puppy, she had been very interested in rabbiting and mousing. Now at over a year old, she was just not interested. The sheep were quite safe.

How different we all are, I thought. Some, like Crosscastle, are restless and seek after riches and power. Others, like Elswith his cousin and her husband William, seek nothing but contentment in their life.

I waved at Dunstan Weard who was silhouetted on the hill for a moment, then turned my horse to the cottage of Elswith's husband, William Larkworthy. A lark rose above me but it didn't sing.

That day in January came back to me abruptly and unkindly as I jumped from Bayard's back and scratched on the door. I had come to tell William the tale of the death of Elswith's killer and to explain to him why his beloved wife had been murdered.

I shivered. I did not relish the task.

Pygge's flesh healed and he entered the priory of St. Margaret of Antioch that spring. He would, as Johannes had prophesied, always walk with a limp.

Do you know what, Paul my lad? The man is happy in the priory still. He's Almoner now.

Tostig and Alysoun were at last married at the door of the church at Durley and off they went happily to their newly refurbished house in the village, that was once lived in by my childhood friend and village carpenter, Martyn. He'd died a terrible death in that awful winter of four months' ice and snow and I still looked for him about the place now and again; before a stab to the heart told me he was no longer in the world.

After he had died we'd found a Saxon prince buried on our land and had dug him up to inter his bones in our village churchyard. The King had taken all this man's trappings and possessions as treasure trove, leaving Lydia with a fine memento - a little enamel apple, which she jealously guarded and valued highly.

Now we were about to discover another ancient site in the forest. We were removing all the charred beams and rubbish from the site of the old Cadley church and would rebuild it in stone.

The villagers were busy about the clearing of the site. Some of my foresters who lived further afield had come to help. Gradually the floor of the temple was revealed. I sat on my horse and watched as the last vestiges of the ruined Saxon church were removed. Johannes stood on the edge looking in.

Throwing my leg over Bayard's head I jumped down and stood by him at the edge of the pit, which now formed the large oblong housing the temple.

The place had been covered with a barrel vaulted roof, naturally now destroyed. The walls were plain stone, unadorned. At the sides were two raised plinths, like the stone seat which ran around the edge of the gaol at the castle. At the eastern end was an altar with a fine carving of the God and his bull. I noticed a small square fossa at one end of the space and wondered what this had been for. I must have voiced my question for Johannes came back with, "I know what it was for."

"What? How?"

"There was a temple of Mithras close by the medical school I trained at in Salerno. I recognise it now. That hole," he pointed to the flagstoned pit, "was for the initiates to stand in whilst warm bull's blood was poured over them."

"Ergh... whatever for?"

"It was rather like our baptism I believe."

"Ah, I see."

"The pictures on the floor are all symbols of the God. The spear with which he killed the ancient beast, the cup which held the blood, the sickle shaped knife with which he cut the bull's throat, the cap which Mithras wore....Well, I think it was...." he said.

"It looks like the cap old Quimper, Robert's tutor wore."

"Yes, a Phrygian cap. Every temple had such images and they all had a statue of the God killing the bull. There were different grades of initiation and the images represented those too, though don't ask me what they were, for I have no idea."

"I think you know quite a lot about this belief, Johannes."

"No, not really, just what I could glean when I was there. I know it was a belief popular with soldiers. Roman soldiers. I expect this temple was something to do with the town of Cunetio, just a mile or so down the valley at Mildenhall."

"Crosscastle told me that the smaller room through that archway there," I pointed to the western end, "was the narthex where the supplicants would wait to be ushered in here and the passage way down there was a service corridor. It makes me wonder what else is buried under our forest, Johannes."

"I once saw a complete house you know. Called a villa. There had been a fall of some ground when we'd had a small earthquake and this place was revealed. Some of us explored. The floors were similar to this. Lots of tiny pieces of stone all made into pictures. So clever."

"You must go into this narthex and look at the twelve astrological signs. They are quite beautiful," I said.

"The floor in one of the rooms of this house was quite simply, I think, the most beautiful thing I have ever seen. Gold, red and black set on a cream background. Leaping fish around the edge and in panels in the middle Orpheus with his lyre. Fantastic animals were picked out in detail all around the border and the most amazing complicated patterns interlacing in each other. You've never seen the like, Aumary."

"This will do me, Johannes," I chuckled.

"Aye, and on our doorstep," he smiled. "What will you do with it?"

"I cannot build over it."

"I was told that the early Christian church built over these places to harness the power of the old gods."

I smiled. "No, I can't do that. I'll build the new church a little way off."

"And this...?" asked my friend, pointing down.

I shook my head. "I think I must cover it over again. Let it lie. I cannot leave it open to the elements."

"Leave it for someone else to rediscover when we are all long gone, eh?"

I chuckled as I turned away. "Let it live on in the memory of those who saw it. That's enough."

Pardon Paul? Oh yes... what happened about the contest? Well, all went on as normal. A year and a day went by....

The Flitch contest was held the following January. Two couples only were left. My forester Osmund and his wife took the prize of the Flitch and the wheelwright and his wife were awarded second prize.

A little while later, William Larkworthy told me that Osmund and Godgifu had offered a half of the Flitch to him, for they felt that they had won unfairly and it should have been William and Elswith winning the prize.

After very little consideration, he told me, he did not accept it.

~ ~ ~ ~ ~

GLOSSARY

Apothecary - Primitive dispensing chemist.

Beltane - The pagan celebration of May 1st, Mayday, when bonfires are lit.

Besom - a twig brush.

Brazier - portable charcoal burning grate.

Cellarer - Person in charge of the food supplies at a monastery or castle.

Chink - coin.

Chitty faced - baby faced, meaning the person is a cowardly youth with no courage.

Coroner - The man appointed by the Crown to deal with unexpected deaths. The Coroner was the man who drew up the jury of twelve men to decide the cause of death and if need be, impose fines.

Crikes - A mild swear word, derived from Christ.

Deerman - the forester who looks after the welfare of the deer.

Distaff - A wooden stick like tool used in spinning. It is designed to hold the unspun fibers, keeping them untangled.

Downs - Chalk hills with steep coombes and valleys, thin soils and few trees.

Dwale - a soporific drink made from deadly nightshade or belladonna.

Fadoodling - Messing about with.

Fellowes - a measure of wood.

Firkin - a small cask formerly used for liquids, butter, or fish.

Flan - Coin blank.

Flitch - A large side of bacon.

Fonkin - mediaeval word for a fool.

Forest Law - The royal forest embraced not only wooded areas, but also large tracts of arable land and even towns and villages. Anyone dwelling or holding land within the forest bounds was subject to a complex set of regulations, implemented by royal officials answerable only to the king. They were prevented from hunting freely but, more importantly, the laws of the vert denied them the right to utilise their land as they saw fit.

Gambeson - A woollen stuffed, wool jerkin, sometimes with short sleeves worn under the chain armour or as a protection in itself.

Garderobe - Primitive toilet built into a wall.

Gilbertine Canons - Founded around 1130 by in Saint Gilbert of Sempringham of Lincolnshire where Gilbert was the parish priest. It was the only completely English religious order. There was a priory in Marlborough town.

Gurt - Huge (Wiltshire dialect).

Gyves - Restrainers for the ankles.

Herald - Royal messengers,courier.

Killcow - A bully.

Mêlée - Uncontrolled fighting. Disturbance.

Midden - Dung heap.

Ostler - A stable man in a public stables.

Pannikin - Small metal pan.

Pattens - Wooden overshoes.

Phrygian Cap - A tight cap which had a pointed top and which was tied under the chin.

Plinth - the base course of a building, or projecting base of a wall.

Rouncey - A smaller horse used as a workhorse often ridden by servants. Rounceys were not fast but they were possessed of great stamina.

Sally Port - Small personnel door in a wall or gate, usually at the opposite side of the wall to the main gate.

Sanctuary - A sacred place, such as a church, in which fugitives were immune to arrest recognized by English law. They had forty days to make up their mind to either plead guilty and go into the hands of the law, or abjure the realm. (Leave never to come back).

Scrip - A pouch worn slung over the shoulder or a smaller one hanging from a belt.

Shuttle - a tool designed to neatly and compactly store the thread across the loom weft yarn while weaving.

Skivvy - a badly used relative usually a woman, who is treated like a slave.

Solar - Generally on an upper storey, a room designed as the family's private living and sleeping quarters. The room was usually situated so that sunlight would be caught for the maximum amount of time in the day.

Spadger - Sparrow.

Sparhawk - Sparrowhawk.

Spinster - Person (usually a woman but not exclusively), who spins thread and yarn with her distaff, by hand.

Stoup - a basin for holy water, especially on the wall near the door of a Roman Catholic church.

Strike-a-light - Small box with tinder and flint with which to make fire.

Vespers - a service of evening prayer in the Divine Office of the Christian Church.

Villein - tied peasant.

Wurry - strangle (Wiltshire dialect).

AUTHOR'S NOTE

The most famous Flitch contest is that held up to this day in the Essex town of Dunmow. Apparently, they were quite common in the middle ages. As far as I know, Marlborough never had such a contest.

There is indeed a Roman road running through the forest of Savernake. Cunetio (Mildenhall) is but a mile to the north and this was a major place in Roman times. It's not hard to imagine that there might have been a villa somewhere close by. There is a wonderful villa close to Hungerford, at Littlecote House, very close to the boundary of the present forest and certainly well within the old one. This villa has a fabulous pavement known as the Orpheus mosaic. It's the largest and most complete Roman villa in the country. Johannes speaks about a pavement which I have based on the Littlecote mosaic.

Temples of Mithras are quite common - there are several in the United Kingdom, the most famous in London and at Carrawburgh near Hadrian's Wall, in the north. I have based my own temple upon the one under the baths of Caracalla in Rome. It was well known that Mithras the Bull Slayer was worshipped in this country by soldiers, in particular, hence the temple on Hadrian's Wall. It was common for Christian churches to be built upon heathen sites; one way to get the populace to accept the new religion.

The present church of Cadley is Victorian and is now deconsecrated and a private home. As far as I know there was never a Mediaeval church here but I am willing to be contradicted. The church I describe is based on the Saxon church at Greensted in Essex and the oldest wooden church in Europe dating to the 7th century, though dendrochronology indicated the present church dates from 1060.

Marlborough did indeed have a royal mint in the Saxon and early Norman reigns. During John's reign, however, there was no mint in the town. We know nothing about the original building for this and the castle no longer exists, except for the keep mound, which is in the grounds of Marlborough College. You must forgive me if I have made it fanciful. Mediaeval mints are rare finds. I thank Dave Greenhaugh (Grunal Moneta), for all the information on the mints and coins of the reign of John and for his help in disentangling an (originally), unworkable plot!

Now to Aumary. He is a minor lord, not terribly wealthy and more a businessman than pure aristocracy. As warden of the forest he has quite a practical job and needs to know about the forest and its trades. He is a knight - yes, but first and foremost, a forester. I have made him a sympathetic character as so many folk of his class are portrayed in novels as proud, haughty and nasty. I fail to see how many of them could be so. They were dependent upon their peasants for their livelihood. If the peasant didn't prosper, neither did they at this level of society. Grander folk perhaps could be less amenable. Aumary takes every man as he finds him and isn't averse to rolling up his sleeves and getting on with it.

Sue Newstead © 2019

ABOUT THE AUTHOR

Susanna, like Aumary Belvoir has known the Forest of Savernake all her life. After a period at the University of Wales studying Speech Therapy, she returned to Wiltshire and then moved to Hampshire to work, not so very far from her forest. Susanna developed an interest in English history, particularly that of the 12th and 13th centuries, early in life and began to write about it in her twenties. She now lives in Northamptonshire with her husband and two small wire haired fox terriers called Delphi and Tabor.

TITLES IN THIS SERIES

Belvoir's Promise

She Moved Through the Fair

Down by the Salley Gardens

I Will Give my Love an Apple

Black is the Colour of my True Love's Hair

Long Lankyn

One Misty Moisty Morning

The Unquiet Grave

The Lark in the Morning

Please visit the website for further information

https://susannamnewstead.co.uk/

Printed in Great Britain
by Amazon